For Manda

(I'm not sure I could have done it without you!) D.M.

First published in 2021 by Nosy Crow Ltd

The Crow's Nest, 14 Baden Place

Crosby Row, London, SE1 1YW

www.nosycrow.com

ISBN 978 1 78800 989 8

Nosy Crow and associated logos are trademarks

and/or registered trademarks of Nosy Crow Ltd.

A CIP catalogue record for this book is available from the British Library.

Printed in China

Papers used by Nosy Crow are made from wood grown in sustainable forests.

10 9 8 7 6 5 4 3 2 1

Ruffles

and the **red**,
red coat

David Melling

This is **Ruffles.**

Ruffles **loves** . . .

singing . . .

scratching . . .

eating . . .

fetching . . .

sniffing . . .

chewing . . .

digging . . .

running . . .

and sleeping.

But Ruffles **does not love** his new coat.

Not one . . .   teeny, tiny . . .   little bit.

No.   No.   No.

No.   No.   No.

Ruffles should wear his coat
when it is cold and wet.

Today, it is cold and wet . . .

and the rain is making puddles.

Ruffles **loves** puddles.

So Ruffles sniffs . . .   and pats . . .   and licks . . .

and splishes . . .   and splashes . . .   and sploshes . . .

and jumps . . .   and jumps . . .   and jumps . . .

without his coat.

Here is Ruffles' friend, Ruby!

Ruby's wearing her smart new coat!

They sniff . . .   and pat . . .   and lick . . .

and splish . . .   and splash . . .   and splosh . . .

and jump . . .   and jump . . .   and jump, until . . .

. . . big dogs come!

The puddle is all sploshed away.

And Ruffles is wet and cold and cross.

But Ruby shakes . . . and wags her tail. She still wants to play!

Ruffles doesn't. No. No.

No. No. No.

Now Ruby is sad.

So she goes away.

And Ruffles is all alone.

But here's Ruby again!
With Ruffles' new coat!

Ruffles will do **anything** for Ruby, even if . . .

it takes . . .   a really long time . . .   and he has to do . . .

lots and . . .   lots of . . .   wriggling.

Until . . .   at last!   The coat is on . . .

. . . and **look!**

Another puddle!

Maybe the new coat is not so bad after all.

Ruffles loves . . .

sniffing . . .   patting . . .   licking . . .

splishing . . .   splashing . . .   sploshing . . .

and jumping . . .   in puddles . . .   but, most of all . . .

Ruffles **loves** . . .

Ruby!